WHALE

OF AN

IDEA

BY: MELISSA CARTER, RICH LINDEMAN, AND KAT SLADE

AuthorHouse™
1663 Liberty Drive
Bloomington, IN 47403
www.authorhouse.com
Phone: 1 (800) 839-8640

Published by AuthorHouse 09/30/2016

ISBN: 978-1-5246-4058-3 (sc)
978-1-5246-4059-0 (e)

Library of Congress Control Number: 2016915585

Print information available on the last page.

Any people depicted in stock imagery provided by Thinkstock are models,
and such images are being used for illustrative purposes only.
Certain stock imagery © Thinkstock.

This book is printed on acid-free paper.

authorHOUSE®

IDEAS CAN BE DARING

Ideas can be Caring

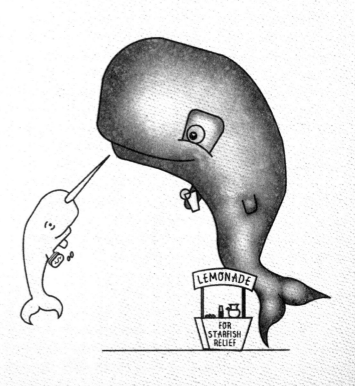

LEMONADE

FOR
STARFISH
RELIEF

Ideas can Locate

IDEAS CAN
CAPTIVATE

IDEAS
CAN PAY
BILLS

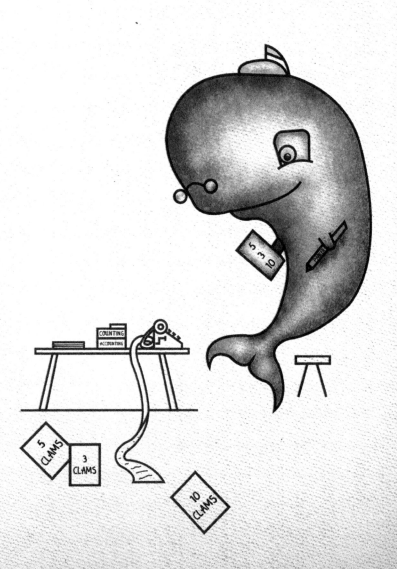

IDEAS CAN CONQUER FEAR

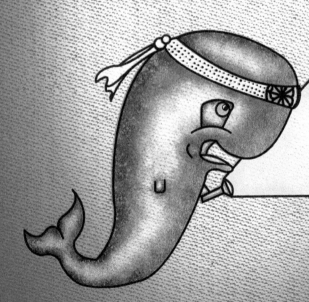

ideas can be
UNIQUE

IDEAS CAN IMPROVE PHYSIQUE

ideas can inspire

ideas can
inquire

Now that they're out,
floating in
the ocean

IDEAS
CAN BENEFIT
SOCIETY

Ideas can have Endless Variety

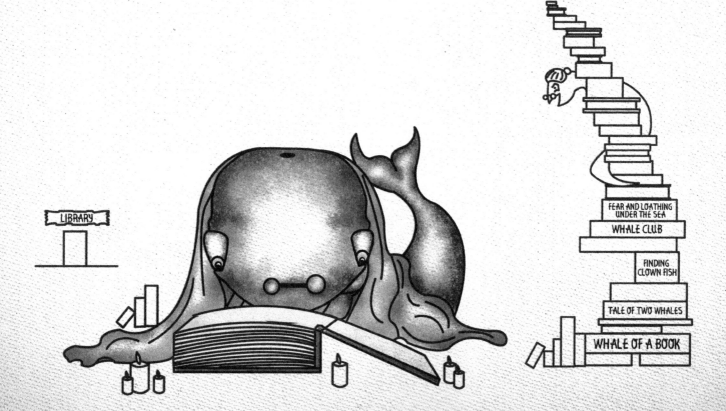

IDEAS CAN COMPETE, BUT BE SURE TO PLAY FAIR

IDEAS CAN BE BUILT WITH QUALITY, LOVE, & CARE

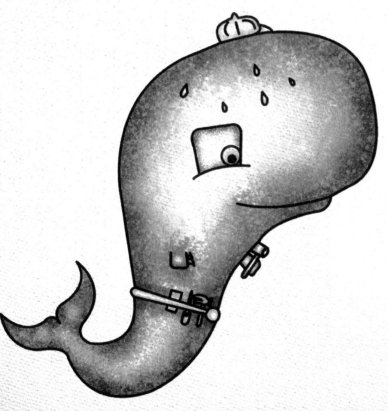

IDEAS CAN BE IMPROVED UPON OR NEW

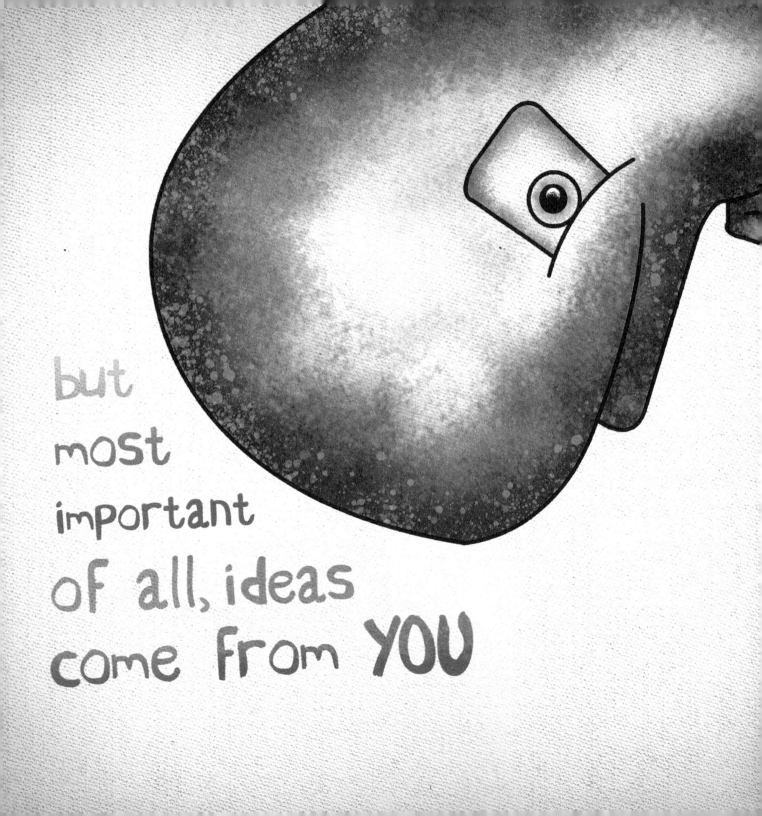

but
most
important
of all, ideas
come from YOU

NOW THAT'S A
WHALE
OF AN IDEA

CPSIA information can be obtained
at www.ICGtesting.com
Printed in the USA
LVOW06s0108081216
516306LV00019B/421/P